Ramadier & Bourgeau

livelifeaberdeenshire.org.uk/libraries

Translated by Antony Shugaar

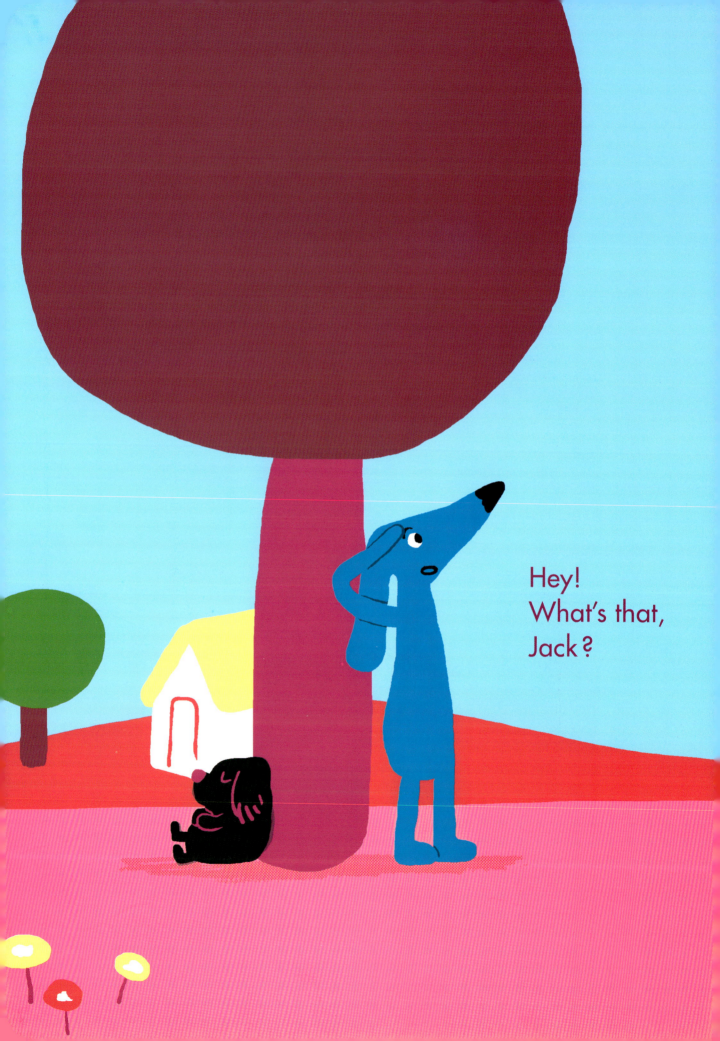

Hey!
What's that,
Jack?

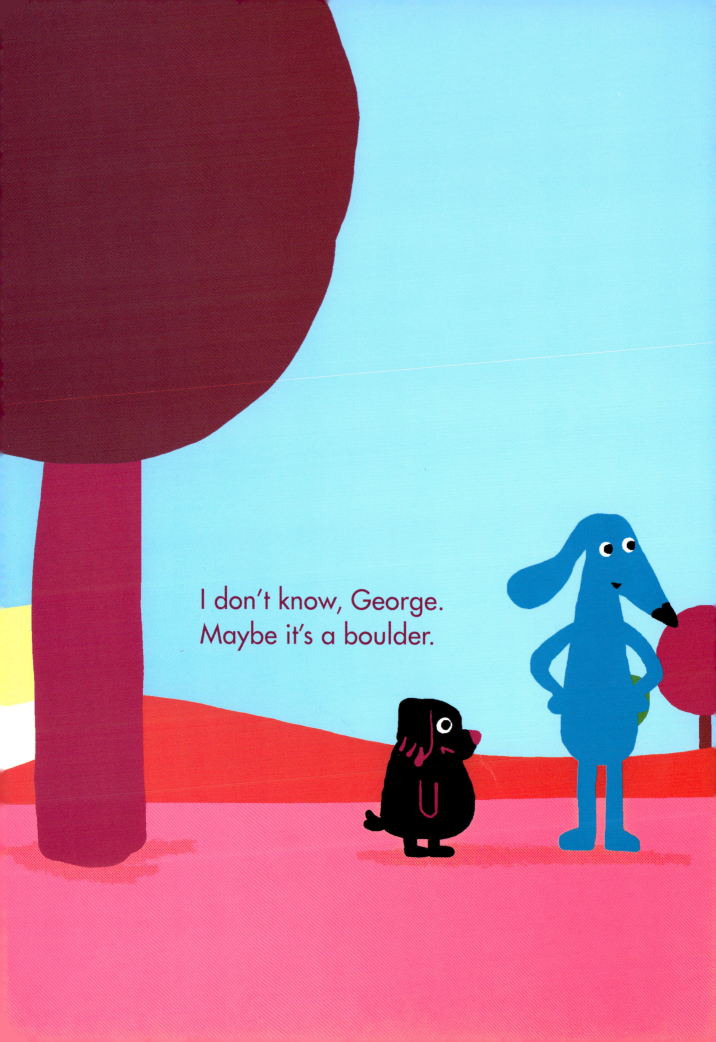

I don't know, George.
Maybe it's a boulder.

It's a bit soft for
a boulder, isn't it?

What is it,
Jack?

I don't know, George,
maybe it's a ball!

You're right, Jack, it's rolling!

It's rolling fast, George!

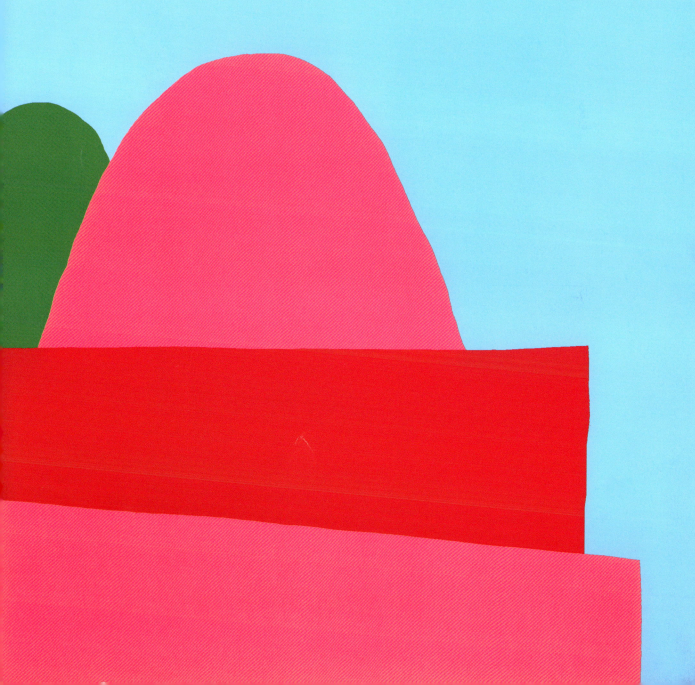

AAAAHHH

Whoa!
What is it,
Jack?

I don't know, George.
It might be a parachute!

What is it,
Jack?

I don't know, George.
It seems to be a raft.

Uh-oh!
What is it,
Jack?

I don't know,
George,
I don't know!

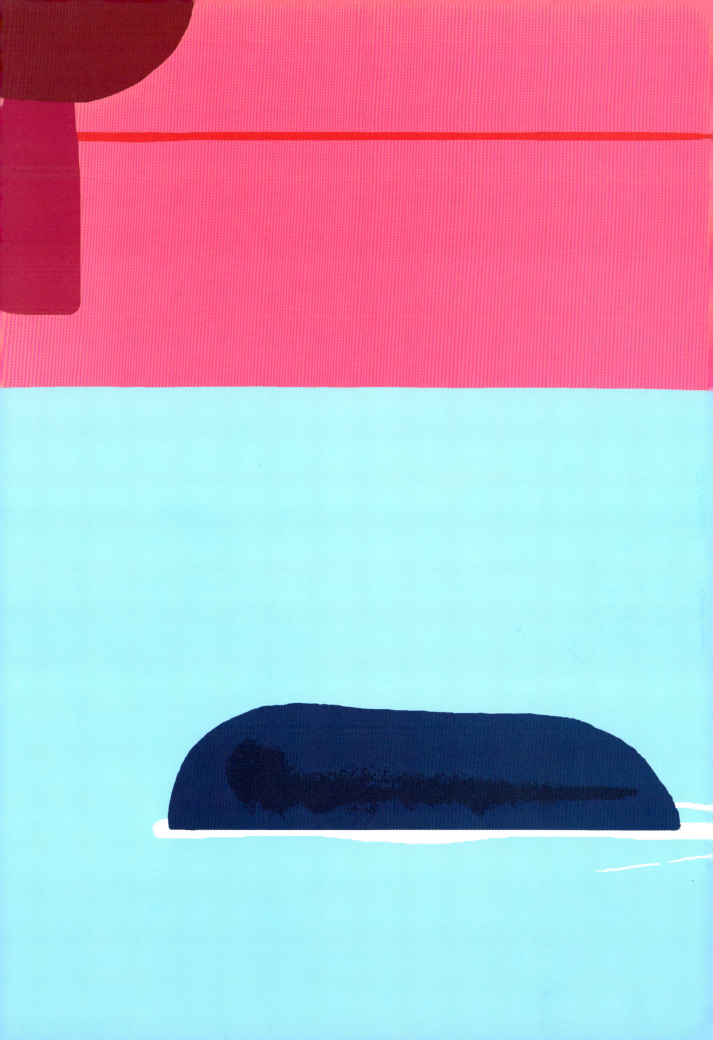

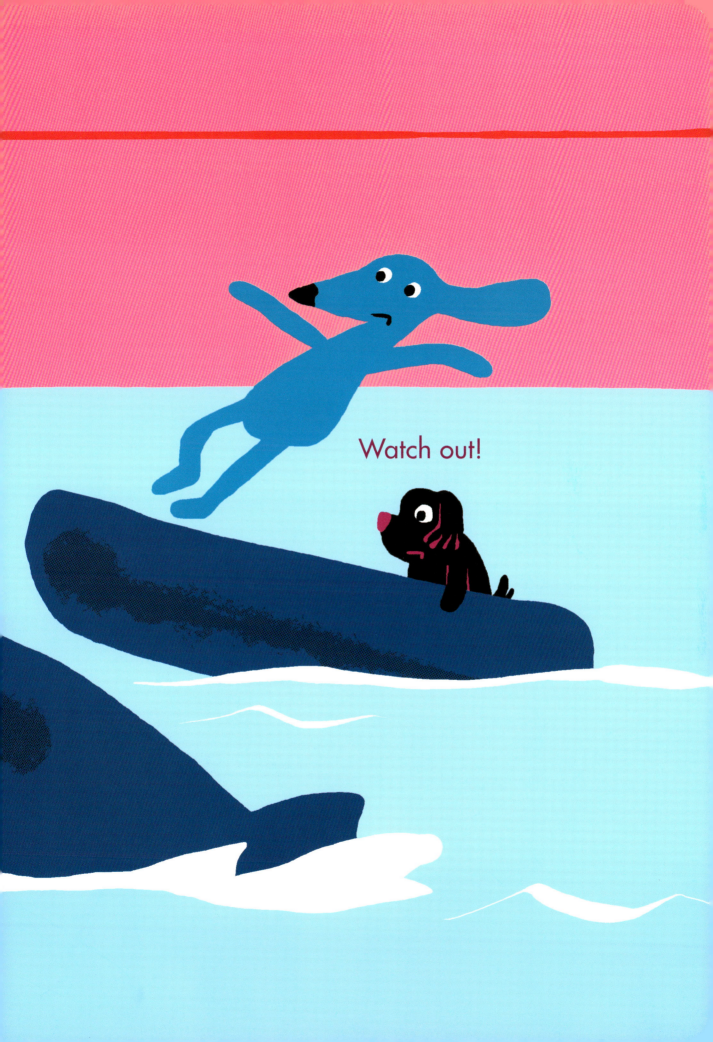

Brrr,
I'm cold,
Jack.

Me too,
George,
me too.